Living Through a Pandemic

A Cut-Out and Coloring Activity Book

Pei Lin and Aaron Dietz

ISBN 978-0-578-86980-3

A few weeks ago, our family learned about a dangerous pandemic. Since then, our lives haven't been the same.

Cut out the family members and other items. Use these cut-outs to play out the story throughout the book.

Cut out the items on the other side of this page.

What color is the house? Whatever color you choose. The packages you cut out can be placed just outside the door.

✂

First of all, we avoid leaving the house as much as possible. Things that we used to go out for, we try to have delivered to us.

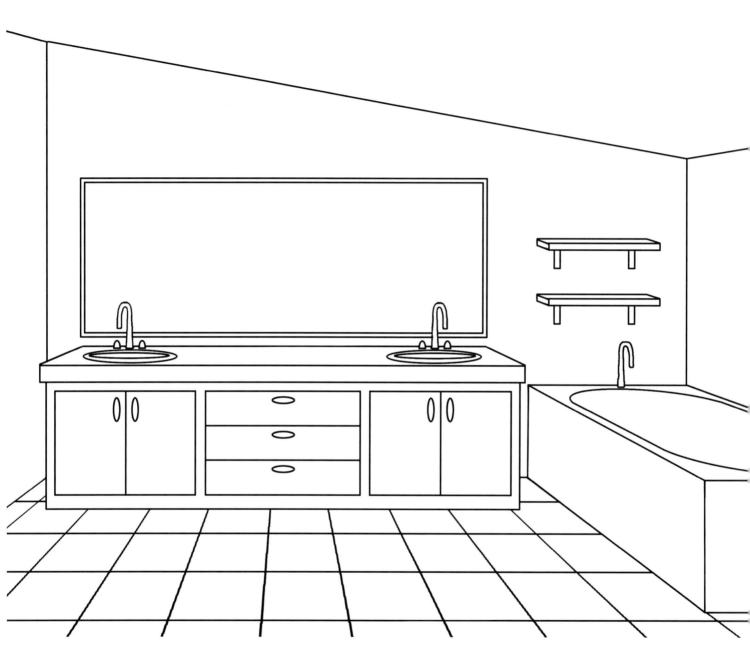

We also make sure to wash our hands often, for twenty seconds each time. That's how long it takes to sing "Happy Birthday" twice.

Put some soap and towels in the bathroom. What do you think they might see when they look in the mirror? You can draw that in!

The grocery bags and masks will come in handy on the next page.

MASK
REQUIRED
TO ENTER

Cut out the items on the other side of this page.

What fruit is in the stand outside? Are they apples, oranges, melons, or something else? Make it the color of the fruit you want. What do you think the grocery has in its windows? You can draw that in!

If we do need to leave the house, we wear masks. Masks help prevent the spread of the disease.

Mom leads a team of software developers. She has been working from home instead of going into the office. We try not to interrupt her work, especially when she's in a meeting.

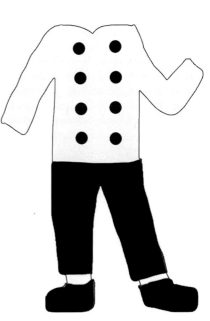

Draw in some books and other items for the bookshelves. Draw some art inside the frame hanging above the desk.

Mom might need the DO NOT DISTURB sign on the door during meetings.

Wear a mask

FACE SHIELD 101X7

SORRY, WE'RE CLOSED

OPEN

Cut out the items on the other side of this page.

Help reopen
the bakery by
drawing your
favorite pastries
on the shelves.

Dad is a pastry chef. His bakery is closed right now but when the trustworthy health officials say it's okay to reopen, he will wear special gear to help people stay safe.

Even though Dad's bakery is closed, he still keeps busy. He cooks, cleans, and tends the garden.

What do you think they should plant in the pots? Draw in your idea!

Cut out the items on the other side of this page.

What do you think they should bake next? Draw it on the counter or create a cut-out of your own!

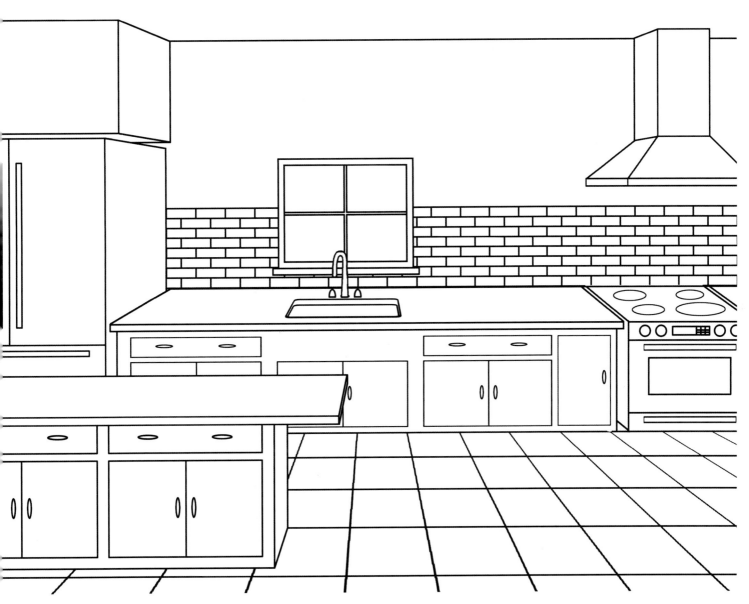

Since we don't go out much, we find things to do around the house. Today, we made cookies to send to my aunt. We made plenty of extra cookies so that we could have some too!

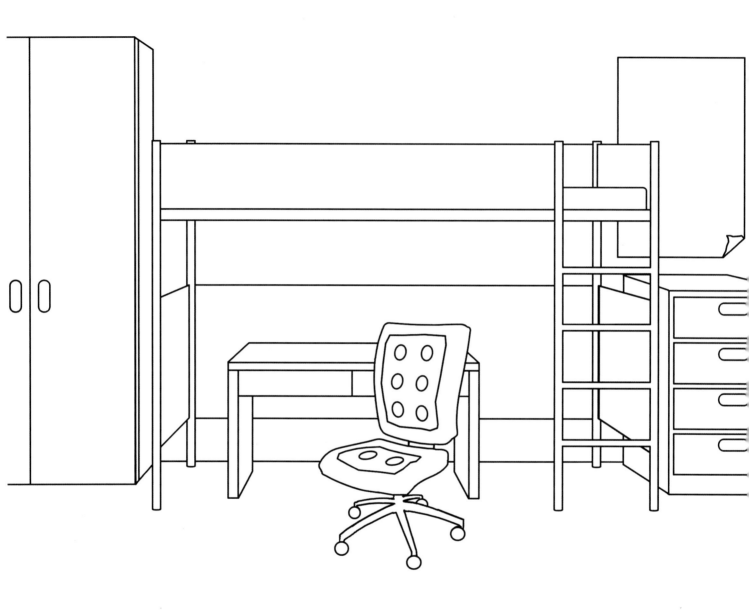

I haven't been to school since the pandemic started, but my teacher still talks to us every day online.

Turn the blank poster into a poster of something that you appreciate. It could be of a favorite scientist, video game, movie, musician, athlete, or whatever else you want it to be!

Cut out the items on the other side of this page.

Mark some
points of interest
on the trail map.
Draw in some
wildlife peeking
out from behind
the trees!

✂

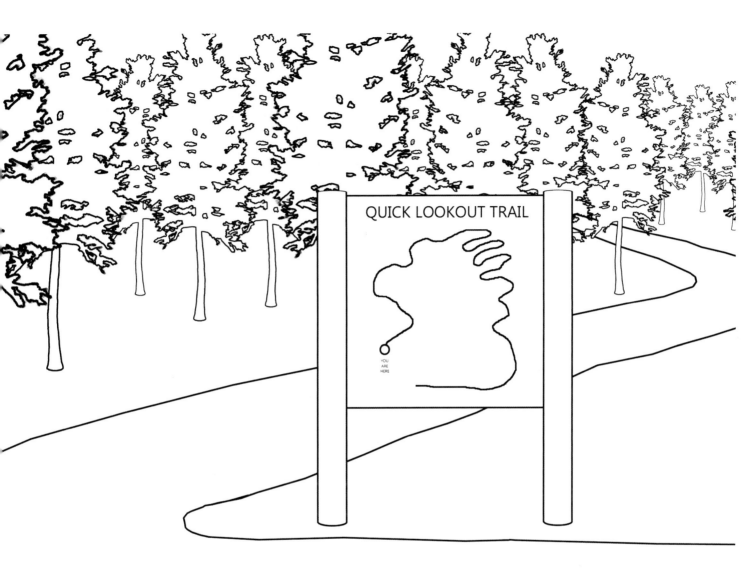

Mom and Dad say it's safe enough to go hiking, as long as we're careful and the trail isn't too busy. We make sure our masks are on when we pass other hikers. It's good to get out of the house for a while!

There are plenty of things to do indoors also. Family game night is almost every night! And most of the time we can wear our pajamas all day.

Add your favorite
board games
to the shelves,
or draw in your
favorite books!

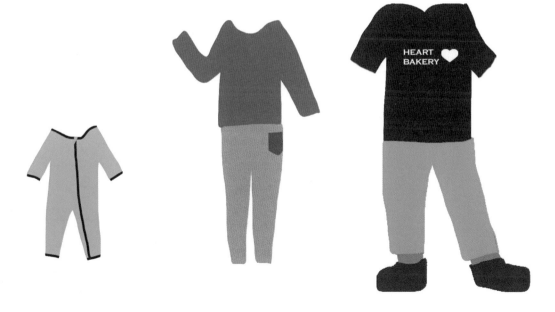

Cut out the items on the other side of this page.

Is it day or night? Is the ball in the sky the sun or the moon? Color it in accordingly. The family may need a small fire in the firepit to stay warm.

✂

Grandma had to cancel her trip to visit us, but we still see her on video calls. When the weather is nice, we call her from our backyard!

After a few weeks of playing the same board games, Mom and Dad changed things up by creating a scavenger hunt. I followed clues hidden all over the house to find all the ingredients to make...more cookies!

Hide a cookie
ingredient under
the bed for the
scavenger hunt.
Draw some art in
the frame above
the bed. Can you
make a cut-out
of a stool or chair
for the vanity?

Cut out the items on the other side of this page.

The family might need some family portraits in the picture frames, or whatever else you think will look nice. Create cut-outs of your favorite foods to add to the dinner table!

✂

Living through a pandemic is tough, but we are grateful that we are together as a family, and that we are able to take steps to stay safe. It helps that we have all the ingredients to bake more cookies!

A **pandemic** is when a disease makes people sick all over the world.

Transmission is how a disease is transferred from person to person. Diseases can be transmitted in different ways. This book describes a pandemic in which the disease can spread through tiny particles that travel from person to person, like when a sick person sneezes and a particle from their sneeze lands on someone else.

Face coverings, or masks, are not 100% effective but can reduce transmission of disease. Wearing a mask means you are doing your part to keep people safe.

The family in this book stays relatively safe during the pandemic because they have the resources and living situations that allow them to reduce their chance of catching the disease. During a pandemic, it's important to support people who do not have these advantages, as well as anyone whose well-being is impacted. Types of support can include donations of financial aid, food, and supplies; counseling; Personal Protective Equipment (PPE); and other assistance. Even offering to pick up a few items from the drug store for a neighbor can help, though you should follow trustworthy health experts' advice when dropping them off to make sure everyone stays safe.

About the Authors

Pei Lin and Aaron Dietz live in Seattle.

On a good day, Pei will bake something delicious, play tennis, eat Taiwanese food, and catch up with her family on a video call, and Aaron will write something decent, play tennis, read a book, and build a data visualization. On the best day, they'll do all of these things while traveling safely in a foreign country.

Made in the USA
Columbia, SC
14 April 2021